PARKER SHINES ON

For my baby brother, Cash man

—P. C.

For my heartbeats, the happy babies, PNC, AAM & MCM II

—J. C.

For my mom, Michelle, who supported me in all phases of my career
and believed in me no matter what. All the sacrifices you've
made have been instrumental in making my dreams come true.
Thank you for being such an amazing woman.

—B. J.

ALADDIN
An imprint of Simon & Schuster Children's Publishing Division
1230 Avenue of the Americas, New York, New York 10020
First Aladdin hardcover edition October 2021
Text copyright © 2021 by Jessica Curry and Parker Curry
Illustrations copyright © 2021 by Brittany Jackson
Photo of Parker Curry on page 48 provided by Jessica Curry
All rights reserved, including the right of reproduction in whole or in part in any form.
ALADDIN and related logo are registered trademarks of Simon & Schuster, Inc.
For information about special discounts for bulk purchases, please contact Simon & Schuster Special Sales
at 1-866-506-1949 or business@simonandschuster.com.
The Simon & Schuster Speakers Bureau can bring authors to your live event. For more information or to book an event
contact the Simon & Schuster Speakers Bureau at 1-866-248-3049 or visit our website at www.simonspeakers.com.
Designed by Laura Lyn DiSiena
The illustrations for this book were rendered digitally.
The text of this book was set in Filson Soft.
Manufactured in China 0721 SCP
10 9 8 7 6 5 4 3 2 1
CIP data for this book is available from the Library of Congress.
ISBN 978-1-5344-5474-3 (hc)
ISBN 978-1-5344-5475-0 (eBook)

PARKER SHINES ON

Another Extraordinary Moment

By **Parker Curry** & **Jessica Curry**

Illustrated by **Brittany Jackson**

With an afterword by *New York Times* bestselling author **MISTY COPELAND**

ALADDIN

New York London Toronto Sydney New Delhi

PARKER CURRY loved being a big sister.

She played dress-up with
her little sister, Ava.

She played piano with
her baby brother, Cash.

And even when Ava ate the last slice of her birthday cake

or Cash scribbled on her drawing,

Parker still loved being with them, especially—

WHEN THEY ALL
DANCED TOGETHER.

"**Dance party!**" Ava announced each time they began. *Yes, dance IS a party*, Parker thought. It was her *outsides* celebrating the way she felt on her *insides*.

At home, Parker sometimes made up her own steps.

But in dance class, she followed
her teacher's every move.

One day, Parker leaped
across the floor, and . . .

she smacked right
into Mira.

"Oops! I'm sorry!" Parker apologized, hopping back.

Mira smiled shyly.

She was new to the class but *not* new to ballet.

Parker loved watching Mira.

Pirouette!

She was amazing!

And when Mira was given the solo in their
upcoming recital, Parker cheered the loudest.

Still, she wondered, would she ever be as good as Mira?
How would she begin?

Just then, Parker looked up,

ALVIN AILEY

REVELATIONS

SOME PEOPLE
DREAM
OF SUCCESS

WHILE OTHERS
WAKE UP
AND WORK
FOR IT.

MISTY COPELAND

ALICIA
GRAF
MACK

Dance

and she knew exactly what she needed to do.
The only way to get better was to . . .

practice, practice, practice.

Plié!

Relevé!

But one day Ava and then Cash joined in, whirling around the room like a cyclone and banging on the piano.

Parker cried, her hands over her ears, "Stop, please stop!"

For the rest of the week, Parker practiced alone in her bedroom, repeating each step over and over and over.

She could still hear her sister and brother dancing and giggling in the playroom.

They just don't understand, Parker thought. *Becoming a real dancer is serious business.*

Early the next morning Parker's mother
pinned a wreath of tiny flowers in her hair.

Even though she had butterflies in her stomach, Parker felt confident.
All she had to do was remember her steps. What could go wrong?

Backstage at the recital, Parker lined up behind Mira and the other dancers in her class, a row of pale pink leotards fidgeting in the dark.

"Shoulders back,
stand tall, everyone,"
said their teacher as
the music began.

The first dancer in line twirled out onto the stage.

Then the next,

and the next.

But when it was time for Mira's solo, her feet
seemed to grow roots, holding her frozen in place.

I'm too nervous!

Scared? *Mira?*

Parker was surprised.

Suddenly, Parker spotted Ava and Cash in the audience,
waving and smiling and practically jumping out of their seats.

At first, Parker was worried they would ruin the recital,
until she heard Ava call out . . .

and she remembered what she loved.

Parker grinned.

"I've got it!" she said, squeezing Mira's hands.

"WE CAN DANCE TOGETHER!"

And so they did:
whirling and leaping across the stage, letting
their outsides celebrate the way they were
feeling on their insides.

JUST LIKE REAL DANCERS.

STORY BEHIND THE STORY

by Jessica Curry Morton

As soon as Parker could stand up, she was wiggling, shaking, and moving her little body to the rhythm of any music her tiny ears could hear.

Before Parker was born, we played her classical music in the womb and marveled at the movements she'd make in response to the beautiful compositions of Tchaikovsky and Minkus. It came as no surprise to us that her favorite books as a baby and toddler focused on ballet, tutus, and anything related to dancing and moving your body. When Parker was eighteen months old, we enrolled her in ballet classes, and even as the youngest aspiring ballerina in her class, she was poised, focused, and eager to have the opportunity to learn more about what would become her greatest passion.

For Parker, dance is the purest expression of the joy and happiness she feels on the inside. Regardless of race, language, age, or class, it connects us all and has a way of inspiring and lifting us up through an exhilarating, shared experience.

Dance is Parker's happy place. Every chance she gets, she invites us (her family—*especially* her little sister and brother) and anyone she meets to join in and experience it together, with her. We hope after reading this book, you'll let your insides shine through to the outside with a little dance—or even a dance party—and discover *your* happy place.

A NOTE FROM MISTY COPELAND

I couldn't help but be moved by the question that's asked in *Parker Shines On*: What does it take to be a *real* dancer?

Yes, practice, practice—and more practice—discipline, and dedication are essential for every dancer. But I discovered that purpose and passion transformed my steps into something magical and meaningful, allowing me to share my truth and connect with people.

Dancing with your heart and sharing the joy that comes from expressing *who* you are, along with the endless possibilities of who you can become—isn't that what being a *real* dancer is all about?

I think so, and I bet Parker does too.

Misty Copeland

Misty Copeland is the first Black female principal dancer at American Ballet Theatre, one of the leading classical ballet companies in the United States.

DANCERS FEATURED IN PARKER'S STORY

RAVEN WILKINSON (1935–2018) was born in New York, New York. She started ballet lessons when she was nine years old with teacher Maria Swoboda. At the age of twenty she became the first Black woman to receive a contract to dance with the Ballet Russe de Monte Carlo, and, during her second season, was promoted to soloist. Other companies Wilkinson danced with were the Dutch National Ballet and the New York City Opera (ballet ensemble).

ALVIN AILEY (1931–1989) was born in Rogers, Texas. He and his mother moved to Los Angeles, California, when Ailey was twelve years old. He was first introduced to dance by the Ballet Russe de Monte Carlo and the Katherine Dunham Dance Company. His formal dance training began with teacher and choreographer Lester Horton. In 1954, Ailey settled in New York to study modern dance with Martha Graham, Hanya Holm, and Charles Weidman, and ballet with Karel Shook. Ailey founded the Alvin Ailey American Dance Theater in 1958. Among the most well-known Ailey dances are *Blues Suite*, *Revelations*, and *Cry*. In 2011 former Alvin Ailey dancer and artistic director Judith Jamison selected Robert Battle to become artistic director, making him only the third person to head the company since its founding.

KAREN BROWN (1955) was born in Augusta, Georgia. She started ballet lessons when she was eight years old with teacher Ron Colton of the Augusta Ballet. Brown spent twenty-two years with the Dance Theatre of Harlem, which was founded by Arthur Mitchell and Karel Shook, as a principal ballerina, featured artist, master teacher, and lecturer. In 2000 she became the artistic director of the Oakland Ballet, the first Black woman in history to direct a ballet company.

DANCERS FEATURED IN PARKER'S STORY

ALICIA GRAF MACK (1979) was born in San Jose, California, and grew up in Columbia, Maryland. She studied at Kinetics Dance Theatre from ages three to twelve and then at the Ballet Royale Institute of Maryland with teacher Donna Pidel. In 2018 she became the youngest person and first woman of color to become director of the Juilliard School's dance division. Mack has danced with the Dance Theatre of Harlem, Alvin Ailey American Dance Theater, Complexions Contemporary Ballet, and Alonzo King LINES Ballet.

MISTY COPELAND (1982) was born in Kansas City, Missouri. When she was very young, Copeland moved with her family to San Pedro, California. While she first danced with her middle-school drill team, Copeland's first ballet classes were at the local Boys & Girls Club. At thirteen she began taking classes with Cynthia Bradley at the San Pedro City Ballet. In 2001 she became a member of the American Ballet Theatre's (ABT's) corps de ballet, the only Black woman in a group of eighty dancers. In 2007 she became the company's first Black female soloist in two decades, and in 2015 she was appointed to be one of ABT's principal dancers, becoming the first Black woman to be named a principal in the company's seventy-five-year history.

Three-year-old Parker Curry,
future ballerina